Pasture Bedtime

Pasture Bedtime

Sigmund Brouwer

illustrated by
Sabrina Gendron

orca Echoes

ORCA BOOK PUBLISHERS

Text copyright © Sigmund Brouwer 2021
Illustrations copyright © Sabrina Gendron 2021

Published in Canada and the United States in 2021 by Orca Book Publishers.
orcabook.com

Library and Archives Canada Cataloguing in Publication
Title: Pasture bedtime / Sigmund Brouwer ; illustrated by Sabrina Gendron.
Names: Brouwer, Sigmund, 1959– author. | Gendron, Sabrina, illustrator.
Series: Orca echoes.
Description: Series statement: Orca echoes
Identifiers: Canadiana (print) 20200182412 | Canadiana (ebook) 20200182439 |
ISBN 9781459825888 (softcover) | ISBN 9781459819153 (PDF) |
ISBN 9781459819160 (EPUB)
Classification: LCC PS8553.R68467 P37 2021 | DDC jc813/.54—dc23

Library of Congress Control Number: 2020931807

Summary: In this partially illustrated early chapter book and the first book in the
Charlie's Rules series, eleven-year-old Charlie tries his hardest to keep his life quiet
and organized amid the chaos of life on the farm with his veterinarian mother.

Orca Book Publishers is committed to reducing the consumption of
nonrenewable resources in the making of our books. We make every
effort to use materials that support a sustainable future.

Orca Book Publishers gratefully acknowledges the support for its publishing
programs provided by the following agencies: the Government of Canada,
the Canada Council for the Arts and the Province of British Columbia
through the BC Arts Council and the Book Publishing Tax Credit.

Cover artwork and interior illustrations by Sabrina Gendron
Author photo by Rebecca Wellman

Printed and bound in Canada.

24 23 22 21 • 1 2 3 4

For Jenna and Lauren and Dees.

Chapter One

Outside the horse barn on a Saturday morning, Charlie lifted his power drill. He pressed the quarter-inch bit against a piece of wood. He was ready to drill hole 85 into board 12. It always felt good to make a perfect hole in just the place it needed to be.

Charlie clicked the trigger.

Nothing happened.

He clicked again. Nothing.

He set the power drill down carefully on a nearby table. He pulled off his protective goggles. He pulled out his foam earplugs.

He wondered if somehow the power drill had come unplugged. He looked behind him. He yelled and jumped. A girl stood three steps away.

"Hey," she said. She held the unplugged end of the drill cord. "Thought it would be easier to talk if you weren't working."

She chewed gum hard as she spoke. She pointed at the foam earplugs. "A little much, don't you think? Goggles and earplugs just to do some drilling?"

The girl was about Charlie's age. Her dark hair was almost to her shoulders, and she had a grin on her face. A big grin. It seemed to light up her brown eyes.

"Who are you?" Charlie asked.

"And seriously," she said. "You have a number on each of the boards. What's that about? And this map thing with numbers. Wait. I get it. The numbers on the boards match the numbers on the map, right?"

"It's called a blueprint. And who are—"

"Did you cut the boards yourself? A power saw would be cool. I can see why you'd need goggles and earplugs for a power saw. Very cool. One slip and you lose a finger or a hand. But goggles and earplugs for a power drill?"

The girl was right about the dangers of a power saw. Charlie wasn't allowed to cut wood by himself. "My dad helped me cut the boards yesterday before he left for the week. Who are you?"

Charlie and his parents and his baby sister, Chloe, lived on a ranch. It wasn't like in the city, where any neighborhood kid could just stop by.

"What are you building, anyway?" the girl asked. Another quick chew of bubble gum. "Must be important."

"A doghouse."

Charlie was proud of his doghouses. He built them, painted them and sold them through his mom's veterinary-clinic website. Somebody had preordered this doghouse. As soon as it was finished, Charlie would get paid.

"A doghouse? You need a map thingy for that?" She snapped her gum.

"Blueprint."

"Seems like you are making this way more complicated than it needs to be. Should be easy to make a doghouse."

"Is your family here with an animal for my mom to see? If you're visiting the clinic, you shouldn't be back here. We have a cattle operation, and this is the ranch area. It can get dangerous. The clinic is in the smaller building you passed on the way here."

"And what about this?" The girl grabbed a pocket-sized notebook from beside the blueprint. "*Charlie's Rules.* Nice handwriting, by the way. Much neater than mine."

"Hey. Put that back."

She flipped to the first page. "*Rule 1: Never trust a heifer. They are the teenagers of the cow world.*" Another pop of gum. "Doesn't make sense to me. What's a heifer?"

"A heifer is a young female cow that hasn't given birth yet." Charlie grabbed the notebook from the girl and slipped it into his back pocket where it belonged. "Maybe you should ask permission before reading someone's stuff?"

The girl rolled her eyeballs. "Why does a person always need to ask permission to do what they want?"

Charlie took a deep breath and spoke slowly. "Who. Are. You."

"Oh." The girl gave Charlie another big smile and stuck her hand out for him to shake. "Amy Ma. No *h* in Ma. I don't like it when people put the *h* in there. Without the *h* it's better. It's like *race car*."

"Race car?" Charlie couldn't keep up.

"Yeah. Race car. A palindrome? Reads the same forward as backward. Like Amy Ma. Easy to remember, right? I'll be twelve in a few months. How old are you? About the same, right? My mom is your mom's

new assistant and bookkeeper. We just got here, and already I'm bored. Is there anything to do out here in the middle of nowhere?"

"The new bookkeeper?" A cold, horrible feeling hit Charlie's stomach. His mom's advertisement had said that the job included lodging in the ranch guesthouse. "You're staying here?"

"Yeah," Amy said. "What I said. By the way, your mom sent me to find you. Something about Mrs. Alred and her dog. It can't move its back legs."

Chapter Two

Charlie loved living on the ranch. He helped his dad with the cattle and assisted his mom in the veterinary clinic. Three red barns stood neatly behind the white ranch house and the smaller white guesthouse. A narrow gravel driveway led from the barns to the houses and then out to the main road. Past all of that was a long view to the horizon, with faraway hills outlined against a hazy sky.

He left the doghouse and jogged up the driveway toward the clinic, hoping Amy would either stay behind or go back to the guesthouse.

She stayed close to him. "A dog that can't move its back legs, huh? That's terrible. Mrs. Alred must be upset."

Charlie didn't answer. If he stayed quiet, maybe Amy would stop asking questions.

The clinic was close to the main road, with a large sign on its big front lawn. The top half of the sign showed the world his mom had university degrees in animal medicine and surgery:

DEMBINSKI VETERINARY CLINIC
DR. SELENA DEMBINSKI, DVM
(Open weekends)

DVM stood for Doctor of Veterinary Medicine.

The bottom half of the sign exposed the world to his mom's horrible sense of humor. All that week, anyone driving by would be tortured with this so-called joke: **RAINING CATS AND DOGS? LOOK OUT FOR POODLES!**

One of Charlie's jobs was to change the joke every Sunday by slotting white plastic letters into place. The previous week a different joke had tormented him: **A DOG GAVE BIRTH NEAR THE ROAD—IT WAS TICKETED FOR LITTERING.**

He pushed open the door and stepped into the clinic waiting room. Amy followed.

Selena stood calmly in her white doctor's coat at the far side of the room, where a chocolate-brown Labrador puppy jumped and barked at her. A woman Charlie had never seen before held the puppy's leash.

"Hello, Charlie," Selena said.

"Hello, Selena," he answered.

In the clinic, when he was working for her, his mom expected him to use her first name. That made him feel grown up. Anywhere else, he called her Mom.

"Sit, Duke!" the stranger yelled. She was an older woman who wore lots of makeup, like she was hoping people would think she was much younger than she was.

The puppy jumped and barked even more.

"See?" the woman said angrily. "This dog is nothing but trouble."

Selena knelt and scratched the puppy's head. The little dog stopped jumping.

"Dogs are social creatures," Selena said. "They want to make eye contact. Because we are so much taller than them, they sometimes jump to get closer to us. Watch this."

She stood. The dog barked and jumped. Selena put her hands to her chest and turned away. "The dog gets no reward for trying to reach me.

He will get attention when he behaves properly."

When the dog settled on all fours, she patted his head and spoke calmly. "Good boy, Duke. Good boy."

Selena stood again. The dog jumped and barked.

"See?" the woman said. "Can't be controlled." She jerked the leash, and the dog yelped and tumbled backward.

"It takes time for a puppy to learn good behavior. Too bad you don't have an older dog to help him stay calm." Selena's voice was quiet and steady. Charlie knew this voice. It meant Selena was trying to control her anger. "When you jerk on the leash like that, it can bruise the puppy's throat."

Amy knelt and stroked the puppy. He remained quiet.

The woman shrugged. "I hate this dog. I bought it for my kids, and they don't take care of it at all. Then it got fleas. And the flea medicine you told me to get makes it foam at the mouth. What kind of clinic is this? You told me to buy the wrong medicine. That's what's hurting the puppy."

"This is certainly strange," Selena said. "But it doesn't seem too serious. How long after you gave him the flea tablet did he start foaming at the mouth?"

"Tablet? Why would I buy a tablet? The liquid was cheaper."

Selena took a deep breath. "The liquid is a topical medicine. That's what you put *on* the dog's body. Not *in* the dog. Tablets are for a dog to eat."

"Nobody told me that," the woman said. "Now you probably poisoned this dog."

"The puppy will be fine," Selena said. "Either use the liquid to bathe the puppy or buy tablets to feed it. The flea problem and the foaming at the mouth will both go away."

"I wish this puppy would go away," the woman said. "I just might send it to an animal shelter. Let *them* worry about the fleas and the barking."

She jerked the leash again, and the puppy yelped louder than before. The woman dragged the little dog out of the clinic. The door slammed behind her.

Selena ran her hands through her hair. "That makes my heart ache."

"Mine too," Amy said. "I wish I could keep the puppy."

Selena smiled. "I feel the same way. But if I kept every animal I felt sorry for, the clinic would be overrun. We do our best to help. That's all we can ever do."

Selena turned to Charlie. "Sorry to take you away from your doghouse. But I'm sure Amy told you about Mrs. Alred. I need to prep a horse for surgery. With your dad away on his cattle-buying trip, I need you to bike over to Mrs. Alred's and be my eyes and ears. I emailed you the questions I'd ask if I was there myself."

"And you'll want me to take a video of her dog too, right?" Charlie asked.

"I could do that," Amy said.

Amy coming along to help. That was the last thing Charlie wanted. The very last thing.

"Charlie usually works by himself," Selena told her.

Charlie wanted to hug his mom. But Selena kept talking.

"However," she said, "I think that's a great idea."

Charlie felt like he had been pushed into a deep, dark hole and was falling and falling.

"Thank you, Dr. Dembinski," Amy said.

"Please, when you are my assistant, call me Selena."

Assistant? The dark hole closed over Charlie.

"Charlie, take Amy with you. She can ride my bike. It will be nice to have an assistant, right?"

Chapter Three

"Did you see the pig poop in time?" Amy asked. "Or did you learn the hard way?"

"What pig poop?" Charlie was annoyed. Why was she ruining a nice bike ride with silly questions?

The two pedaled side by side on the quiet country road. It was a warm day. Charlie had been enjoying the sounds of the birds in the trees and thinking about finishing the doghouse.

"Rule 12: Pigs never poop when walking, so when they stop, watch out."

Charlie braked his bicycle. Amy almost ran into him. "Whoops!" she sang out. "What's going on?"

Charlie hopped off his bike. He leaned it against his leg and unzipped the bag on the bike's handlebar. He pulled out his notebook and pen from a side pocket. He flipped through the pages. *Rule 57: All it takes to bribe an animal is food.*

On the lines below, he wrote slowly and carefully: *Rule 58: Make sure girls who chew bubble gum never again get hold of this notebook.*

He put the notebook and pen back in the side pocket where they belonged. He zipped the pocket shut. Then he zipped the bag shut.

"Let me guess," Amy said. "Rule 58 is about me."

Charlie frowned. She remembered how many rules there were? He unzipped the bag. He unzipped the side pocket. He pulled out the notebook and pen and flipped to rule 58 to make an addition. He wanted to add seven exclamation marks so that it looked like this: *Make sure girls who chew bubble gum never again get hold of this notebook!!!!!!!*

But that wouldn't be the proper use of punctuation. So he only added one exclamation point. *Make sure girls who chew bubble gum never again get hold of this notebook!*

It didn't feel strong enough. He underlined it. *Make sure girls who chew bubble gum never again get hold of this notebook!*

Writing it that way followed punctuation rules *and* felt satisfying. Charlie replaced the notebook and pen, rezipped everything and started pedaling again.

Amy rode along beside him.

"Single file on roads," Charlie said. "It gives cars as much room as possible to go around us. That's what you're supposed to do. It's as important as wearing a helmet."

Which, of course, they were. It bothered Charlie that Amy hadn't fully tightened the strap on hers.

"When I hear a car, I'll drop behind you and make it single file," Amy answered. She popped a few gum bubbles. "Until then we can talk. And I'd still like to know. Rule 12. Did you learn the hard way? How big is pig poop anyway?"

"I'm not interested in talking about pig poop," Charlie said.

"What kind of poop do you like talking about? Kind of weird that you'd have favorite poops."

Charlie would have closed his eyes in frustration, but that wouldn't be safe while pedaling a bike.

"Hey," he said. "Do you hear that?"

Amy tilted her head. About ten seconds later, she said, "Hear what?"

"Silence," Charlie said. "*That's* one of my favorite things. Let's listen for it again. For a lot longer."

Amy laughed. "I like you. Maybe this is going to turn out way better than I thought. I didn't want to move here, you know. I wished my mom and dad would have stayed together. Mom says we have to make the best of it. The guesthouse is nice. And I liked holding that puppy. Must be great to help animals. Except for when you can't. It makes me so sad that the puppy is with a mean woman who might give it to a shelter. How do you feel about that, Charlie?"

"Remember, my mom says all we can ever do is our best to help."

"And if it isn't good enough?"

"All we can ever do is our best to help."

Amy rode in silence for a while. Charlie was just getting back into thinking about the doghouse when she spoke again.

"So," Amy said, popping another bubble. "Did you step in the pig poop or not?"

Chapter Four

It took about a half hour of riding to reach the edge of town where Mrs. Alred lived in a small house with a neat yard surrounded by a white fence. Charlie had done this bike ride many times. He visited Mrs. Alred once a week to cut her lawn and help her with Oscar, her dog.

Charlie leaned his bicycle against the fence.

Amy dropped her bicycle on the grass.

Charlie picked up Amy's bicycle and leaned it against the fence, just down from his.

"Wait," he called. After all, wasn't he in charge? But by the time he had taken his phone from the side pocket of his handlebar bag, Amy was at Mrs. Alred's front door.

"Wait," Charlie said again. He clutched his device, nervous about dropping it.

Too late. Amy had already knocked.

Charlie reached the front steps as Mrs. Alred opened the door. Mrs. Alred had short gray hair. Usually she wore a bright smile, but today, Charlie noticed, she looked tired.

"Hello," Amy said cheerfully. "You must be Mrs. Alred. I'm Amy, Dr. Dembinski's new assistant."

"I love how polite you are, Amy," Mrs. Alred said. "And a new assistant to Dr. Dembinski. How nice for her—and for Charlie!"

"Actually," Charlie said, hurrying up the walk, "Amy is *my* new assistant. And—"

"I'm so glad you're here," Mrs. Alred said. "Please come in."

"Thank you," Amy said.

Charlie followed them inside and into the living room, where the walls were covered with framed photographs.

"Mrs. Alred, your home is beautiful," Amy said. "Who are the people in all these pictures?"

They didn't have time for this, Charlie thought. He had a job to do. He touched his phone's screen and opened the email from Selena.

"The pictures are of my children and grandchildren," Mrs. Alred said. She smiled. "Thank you so much for asking."

"What are their names, Mrs. Alred?" Amy asked. "You must be very proud of them."

"Please," Mrs. Alred said. "Call me Dorothy. And where are my manners? I need to make us some tea. Then I'd be happy to tell you their names."

Charlie frowned. Mrs. Alred had never asked *him* to call her Dorothy. She never made tea for him either. Anyway, who had time to waste learning the names of people they would never meet?

"Where's Oscar?" Charlie asked.

Mrs. Alred's smile faded. "He's in the kitchen. Sleeping. Poor thing. Maybe we should let him get his rest."

Charlie looked into the kitchen. Oscar, a big brown dog with gray in his muzzle, lay sleeping on his mat near the back door.

"Amy, remember that Selena wants you to shoot video on your phone," Charlie said.

"Later," Amy replied. "Mrs. Alred is going to make us tea."

"Fine. I'll shoot the video."

"Join us for tea," Amy said.

"No, thanks."

Charlie used his own phone to record Oscar as he slept. He took a close-up of Oscar's chest so that his mom could tell if Oscar was breathing normally.

Then Charlie returned to the living room. He pointed the phone at Mrs. Alred. "Selena has questions for you. She wants me to record your answers just as if you were speaking to her at the clinic."

He pushed *record*. "Can you describe Oscar's symptoms for me?" he asked.

Charlie felt important. Like a real veterinarian.

"There's not much more I can tell you," Mrs. Alred said. "He's been moving slower and slower, and then this morning I found him dragging himself across the floor. He could only stand on his two front legs. His back legs wouldn't move."

"Has he changed his eating habits?" Charlie asked. This was one of his mother's questions. Then he added something that was not on the list.

"Oscar looks overweight. If he is an old, fat dog, then—"

"*Old and fat*?" Mrs. Alred put her hand to her mouth and started to cry.

Maybe it would be better to stick to questions on the list, Charlie thought. "Mrs. Alred, has Oscar been going to the bathroom regularly?"

Mrs. Alred turned to Amy. "I don't know what I'll do if we have to put Oscar down."

Amy sat beside Mrs. Alred and put a hand on her shoulder.

"Some people find it easier if they get a puppy right away," Charlie said.

Mrs. Alred began to sob.

Amy hugged Mrs. Alred. She looked at Charlie.

"Charlie," Amy said, "maybe you should go check on Oscar. Again."

Charlie didn't like that Mrs. Alred was crying. He was glad he could return to the kitchen and do something that might actually help.

Chapter Five

There were three reasons Charlie used screws to put boards together instead of nails. The first was that when you pounded a nail all the way in, the hammerhead often marked up the board. Or sometimes you missed the nail, and the hammerhead left entire circles in the wood. Marks like that showed sloppy construction.

The second reason was that when nails were near the end of a piece of wood, the wood could split.

The third reason was the fun of using a power drill.

It took extra work, though, to prepare. That was why he had drilled and numbered 225 holes the day before. His father had taught him that if you drilled a screw into a smaller hole already in the board, the board would never split.

He was ready to assemble his boards and make another perfect doghouse. All the boards were arranged on a blanket on the ground to keep the wood from getting smudged with dirt. He had the screws in a box near the power drill. He had his safety goggles and his earplugs. He had his blueprint to make sure each numbered board would be attached in the proper order.

He reached for his earplugs.

Too late.

"Hey, Chuck!"

Charlie groaned and turned. "My name is Charlie."

Amy popped her gum. "Then why did you answer me when I just called you Chuck?"

"What is that?" Charlie pointed at the wagon Amy pulled behind her. It was filled with boards of different sizes and shapes.

"Happy to help with your education," she said. "It's a wagon. It has wheels and a handle. You pull it because it makes things easier to move. I thought if you were working out here, I might as well join you and do my own work."

"Why do you have scraps of wood in the wagon?"

"I told you. It's easier that way. It would be silly to carry them here one at a time."

Charlie told himself to talk in calm, low tones, the way Selena did when she was controlling her anger.

"And what are you going to do with the wood?"

"They're pieces left over from the boards your dad cut for you. Your mom said I could have them. She also told me I could take some nails and borrow a hammer. This is going to be fun. Plus I could use the money from selling a cathouse."

"Cathouse?"

"Or maybe a couple of birdhouses," Amy said. "Or maybe both. Depends on how many boards the cathouse takes."

"You don't know what you're going to build?"

"I'll figure it out as I go." Amy popped her gum. "By the way, I'm going to start my own notebook now. AMY'S RULES. What do you think about that?"

"I think I have a doghouse to build," Charlie said. "I'm going to put in my earplugs."

Maybe she would take the hint, he thought. Maybe she would stop talking and let him finish the things on his list.

It was Sunday. Sign-changing day. At 3:00 p.m. he was scheduled to put up this week's horrible new pet pun on the road sign: *Cuddling A Cat Usually Leaves You Feline Good.*

"Earplugs? No problem. I'll yell. But first let me tell you about Duke."

"Duke?" Charlie asked.

"Remember? The puppy with the mean owner? I checked the website of the local animal adoption center to see if the owner meant what she said.

43

About getting rid of Duke. And she did. Duke is in the shelter. Waiting to be adopted. You know what happens to an animal if no one adopts it, right?"

"I'm sure someone will adopt him," Charlie said. "Now, if you don't mind, I need to build a doghouse."

He put in his earplugs. He put on his safety goggles. He grabbed the boards numbered 1 and 2 and placed them together. The clock was ticking. If he stood around listening to Amy, he would never get anything done.

He grabbed the power drill, but before he could pull the trigger, his mom came around the corner. "All right, you two," she said. "Time for my assistants to join me on a drive. We're off to see Jim Langton. He called to say he's got a cow stuck halfway up a tree."

Chapter Six

They bounced along a gravel road in Selena's truck, splashing through puddles from a rainstorm the night before. Charlie was in the front. He pulled *Charlie's Rules* from his back pocket. The bouncing might make his handwriting messy, but he couldn't wait any longer.

He began. *Rule 59.*

Charlie never wrote *Rule* ~~*Number*~~ *59.* You didn't need the word *number* in

front of a number. Once people saw the number itself, they didn't need it explained.

He continued and finished. *Rule 59: Cows can't climb trees.*

He put the notebook back into his pocket and looked out the window. The landscape was rolling hills with a mix of clumps of trees and the open green pasture where cattle grazed.

Amy sat in the back, directly behind Charlie.

"Selena, I'm worried about Mrs. Alred," Amy began. "She is so sad. Do you have any idea yet why Oscar can't move his back legs?"

"I'm afraid I don't," Selena said. "I passed the symptoms along to a specialist. He doesn't think anything can be done. But Mrs. Alred is going to drive to the city tomorrow so he can examine Oscar. There's a slight hope that he might find a way to help them both."

"Both?" Charlie said. "Is Mrs. Alred sick too?"

"Charlie," Selena said, "Amy is right. Mrs. Alred is very worried about Oscar. She doesn't have anyone else to keep her company. Helping Oscar helps her too."

Charlie saw a sign ahead. *Langton Cattle Company.*

Selena slowed the truck and turned up a driveway lined with trees on both sides. Ahead were a house and a barn by a steep hill overlooking a creek.

"Everybody knows that dogs don't live for more than fifteen or twenty years," Charlie said. "Oscar's getting old, and of course he's going to die.

Wouldn't Mrs. Alred expect that when she first got him as a puppy?"

"The thing is, humans connect through the heart," Selena answered. "What we know doesn't always change how we feel."

"A brain is for logic," Charlie said. He crossed his arms. "And my brain is telling me that cows can't climb trees. It's impossible. Maybe the tree fell over and the cow got stuck in it."

But when they arrived at the Langton barn, there it was, on the bank of the creek. A cow stuck on the thick branch of a huge oak tree. With her calf below, on the ground, bawling for its mom. The mom cow mooed back to the calf and kicked her dangling legs.

Chapter Seven

"Craziest thing I've ever seen," Mr. Langton said.

The group of four stood near a tractor with a forklift attachment on the front.

"Cows can't climb trees," Charlie said.

"Maybe not," Mr. Langton said. He had a wide face and a friendly smile, and his coveralls were marked with dirt. He lifted his cap and scratched his bald head. "Except it's there right in front of us. I'd be okay with a tree-climbing cow if she also knew how to get herself back down. She's so upset, I'm afraid she's going to hurt herself."

Mr. Langton had to raise his voice to be heard above the bawling of the calf and the mooing of the cow. "And that calf hasn't moved from the base of the tree for hours. It's getting hungrier and hungrier and is crying for milk. I can't get my tractor in too close in case I hurt it. And I don't want to rope the poor calf. It's already under enough stress."

"What do you want to do with the tractor?" Amy asked.

"I want to raise the forklift above the cow," Mr. Langton answered. "And then I can climb the tree and run some wide straps under the cow's belly and attach them to the forklift. I should be able to lift the poor animal high enough to clear the branch and then set her down. Except the cow is too worked up right now. She'll be kicking like crazy if I try to lift her. She might injure herself."

"You were right to ask if I could bring some medicine to calm her down," Selena said. "This shouldn't be too tricky once we get the cow nice and dozy. Same for the calf."

"Cows can't climb trees," Charlie said. He pulled out his notebook. This was twice now in two days that he'd needed to underline something.

Rule 59: Cows can't climb trees.

No need for an exclamation point. This was a simple statement of fact. Except there was a cow in a tree right in front of him.

"Well," Selena said, "at least I know what I'm going to say to the cow after I give her an injection to make her sleepy."

"What?" Mr. Langston asked.

"Pasture bedtime," she answered.

It took Mr. Langston a few seconds to understand. Then he roared with laughter. Amy laughed too.

Charlie was not amused. He ignored the pun and the laughter. He told himself again that cows couldn't climb trees.

"Come on," Amy said to Charlie. "Grab your phone, and let's video this from the hill. We can look down at the cow. It will be cool."

"Selena might need our help," Charlie said.

"Nope," Selena said. "I have a dart gun for this. I just need to make sure I have the right doses for each dart. The cow and calf will be calm very soon."

Charlie and Amy climbed the steep hill. It wasn't easy, because the grass was slippery from the previous night's rain. They reached a spot that overlooked the oak tree and the creek.

Through the leaves and branches, they watched as Selena approached the calf with her dart gun. Charlie started to record. He knew the dart gun would make a nice *phhht* sound, but they couldn't hear it because of the mooing and bawling. On video he captured Selena pointing the dart gun at the calf, then reloading and pointing it at the cow.

"It only takes a few minutes," Charlie told Amy.

Sure enough, soon the calf began to wobble. It stopped bawling and slowly sank to its knees. Right after that the cow was quiet too.

Mr. Langton drove the tractor close and raised the forklift high. He turned off the tractor engine and grabbed a few straps from the back. He waved at Charlie and Amy. "I'm a movie star!"

Amy yelled back, "You certainly are, Mr. Langton!"

She turned to Charlie and said, "He's going to climb the tree. I hope he doesn't fall."

"We're the ones who need to be worried about falling," Charlie answered. "I'm worried about this slippery grass. We're so close to the edge of the hill we could land right on top of—"

He stopped.

Amy had the same thought.

"On top of the cow," she finished.

"Look at the branches at the top of the tree," Charlie said. "The smaller ones are broken."

"Look at the marks in the hillside," Amy said. Narrow, deep grooves showed where the cow's hooves had slid.

"Cows can't climb trees," Charlie said.

"But they *can* fall into trees," Amy added.

They gave each other high fives for solving the mystery. And for a moment

Charlie thought it might not be bad to have Amy as an assistant.

Then she said, "So tell me. Rule 12. Did you actually step in the pig poop?"

Chapter Eight

The next Sunday Amy sat with Mrs. Alred on a velvet couch in her living room, and Charlie and Selena sank deep into large soft armchairs. All four people held cups of tea.

Mrs. Alred's eyes were puffy from crying. "I am going to miss Oscar so much."

Amy leaned over and hugged Mrs. Alred. "I can't imagine how much

you are going to miss him. I am so, so sorry for you."

Amy started crying, and they hugged more. Selena moved from the armchair and sat on the couch and hugged them both. Mrs. Alred began to sob.

Charlie didn't understand. Why help someone cry more? Why not find something else to do, so that nobody needed to think about what was happening?

"Maybe I should get the wagon," Charlie said.

Nobody seemed to hear him.

Charlie went outside. He was happy to be away from the crying. He pulled the wagon around to the back of the house, then went up the back stairs and into the kitchen.

Oscar lay on his mat. He whined, as if trying to say hello. Usually Oscar thumped his tail to say hello. But Oscar couldn't move. Not his tail or his legs or even his neck. Soon he wouldn't be able to move his lungs either. Already Oscar was struggling to breathe.

The specialist had not been able to give a reason for Oscar's sickness. All he could tell Mrs. Alred was that Oscar was an old dog and sometimes these things happened. He said that if Oscar got worse, the best thing would be to let Selena give him an injection so he could die without pain.

Charlie returned to the living room. He needed help lifting Oscar into the wagon. Then they would pull Oscar to Selena's truck and lift the wagon into the back for the drive to the clinic.

"Ready?" Charlie asked.

"I can't do it," Mrs. Alred sobbed.

"I understand," Selena said. "We'll come back when you are ready."

"No," Mrs. Alred managed to say. "I know it needs to be done. It's just that I can't be there when it happens. I want to say goodbye to Oscar here. Can I be alone with him before you take him away? Would that be okay?"

"Of course," Selena said. "We'll wait here."

Amy helped Mrs. Alred up from the couch, and they went into the kitchen.

Charlie looked at his watch. If this didn't take too much longer, they could get back to the clinic in time for him to get the tasks on today's checklist completed before supper. He would switch the letters on the road sign and then put together the last half of his doghouse.

For once he wouldn't mind the week's new pun. That was because he had helped solve the mystery of the cow that looked like she had climbed a tree. This week people driving by the clinic would read **WHAT A COW TELLS A SLEEPY CALF: IT'S PASTURE BEDTIME.**

Charlie looked at his watch again and frowned. Why were Amy and Mrs. Alred taking so long in the kitchen?

Finally Amy returned. "Mrs. Alred has gone for a long walk. She asked us to wait a few minutes so she doesn't have to see us lift Oscar into the back of the truck."

"Maybe she could get another dog," Charlie said. "I told her that once. She didn't seem to listen."

Selena smiled sadly at Charlie. "I know you are doing your best to help in your own way. Sometimes, though, it helps to try to imagine what other people are feeling instead of thinking about what needs to be done."

Amy began to cry. "Selena, Mrs. Alred also asked if I would hold Oscar when you give him his last shot. She doesn't want Oscar to be alone when he goes."

"That's fine, if you feel you can do it," Selena said.

"I do," Amy answered.

Charlie remembered his mother's words. *Sometimes it helps to try to imagine what other people are feeling instead of thinking about what needs to be done.* Charlie pictured Amy holding Oscar as the dog died.

He felt his own tears. "Maybe I can be there too?" he asked.

Selena gave him a smile and hugged him.

Chapter Nine

At the clinic Selena and Charlie and Amy carefully lifted the wagon out of the back of the truck. They had placed a blanket at the bottom for padding. Another blanket covered Oscar to keep him warm.

As they set the wagon on the ground, Oscar whined quietly.

"Oh, Oscar." Amy patted Oscar's head. He turned his big brown eyes toward her. Amy looked at Selena. "Tell me again that it won't hurt him."

"We will take him straight to one of the rooms at the back of the clinic," Selena said. "It's painted in soft colors, and the curtains will be drawn so it's not too bright. We will play nice, soothing music. Oscar will barely feel the needle. And then, for him, it will be like falling asleep. And his pain will be over."

Amy gulped and blinked back tears. "I can't stand this."

Charlie didn't like it either.

"It's never easy," Selena said. She gave Amy a hug.

Amy blinked back more tears.

Charlie liked it much better when Amy was popping gum. He liked it much better when he could think about building a doghouse.

As they opened the door to the clinic, a woman drove up in a van.

The tires screeched when she stopped. "Dr. Dembinski!" she called out her open window. "You need to help Buttons!"

"Cheryl, come in!" Selena said. "I'll be just a few minutes with something else. I promise you won't need to wait long."

The woman hurried out of the van. She wore blue jeans and a black T-shirt. Her dark hair was piled in a large bun. She carried a small gray kitten that gave out pitiful meows. "Please," she said. "Can you just take a look? Buttons is in horrible pain."

"It's fine," Amy told Selena. "Oscar and I can wait."

Selena unlocked the door to the clinic. Amy pulled the wagon into the waiting room and sat on the floor beside Oscar. Selena held the door open for Cheryl and Buttons. Charlie followed them all inside.

Cheryl didn't even sit. She held Buttons out to Selena. "Poor little thing. She can't move. She's panting. Her paws are always wet."

Another animal that couldn't move, Charlie thought. What was going on?

Buttons gave another pitiful meow.

"When cats are too hot," Selena told Cheryl, "they sweat through their paws. They pant to try to release the heat. Buttons is heat-stressed." Selena turned to Charlie. "Charlie, would you mind getting us a—"

"A spray bottle from the cupboard, filled with cool water?"

Charlie knew that when a cat was heat-stressed, it helped to wet its fur. That was why cats licked themselves on hot days. When their saliva evaporated, it helped cool them. Just like sweat cooled humans.

Selena smiled and nodded.

Heading to the cupboard and sink at the back of the clinic, Charlie passed Amy, who was stroking Oscar's side. When he returned a short while later with a full spray bottle, Amy was frowning.

"Charlie," she said. She pointed at Oscar's side. "Look at this."

"In a second," he said. He'd been given a job to do.

He returned to Selena and Cheryl and Buttons.

"We'll have Charlie here spray Buttons with a nice mist," Selena explained to Cheryl. "This will help Buttons cool down. Then we'll try to figure out why the poor thing is overheated."

Selena held Buttons out with both hands. Buttons made a tooting sound. From her rear end.

Charlie knew the proper term for it was *flatulence*. What it really meant was that Buttons had just farted. It wasn't a loud fart, but then Button was only a kitten.

"Hmm," Selena said. "Her belly does seem swollen. Let me try something here."

Selena gently squeezed Buttons. The kitten tooted again. And again. Moments later Buttons began to purr.

"Well," Selena said to Cheryl. "That seems to solve the problem. Poor thing was having digestive troubles. Have you been giving Buttons milk?"

"Never. I know milk isn't good for cats."

"Strange," Selena said. She squeezed again, and Buttons tooted again.

Cheryl snapped her fingers. "Cheese! While I was making breakfast, Buttons jumped onto the kitchen table and gobbled up some cheese."

Selena nodded and handed Buttons to Cheryl. "Lactose intolerance. Buttons should be fine if you make sure to keep her away from dairy products."

"Thank you!" Cheryl said. "My purse is in my car."

"How about instead of paying me, you make a donation to the local animal shelter?"

"I'll be happy to do that. Again, thanks!"

As soon as the door closed behind Cheryl, Amy said, "I found something weird on Oscar. Come look."

Selena and Charlie knelt beside the wagon.

Amy pulled aside some of Charlie's fur, revealing a dark red bump the size of a marble. With tiny legs.

"When I was petting him," Amy said, "I felt the bump."

"That's a tick," Selena said. "It's been feeding for some time. We might even find other ticks." Then Selena grinned. "I don't want to make any promises, but by keeping us from taking Oscar to the back of the clinic, that little kitten may have just saved Oscar's life."

Chapter Ten

After lunch Charlie began switching letters on the road sign. **WHAT A COW TELLS A SLEEPY CALF: IT'S PASTURE BEDTIME.**

Two drivers honked at him as he finished. One gave him a thumbs-up. Normally Charlie wondered how other people could actually enjoy these puns, but in this case, he agreed and gave the driver a thumbs up in return.

All that was left on his checklist was to finish building his doghouse.

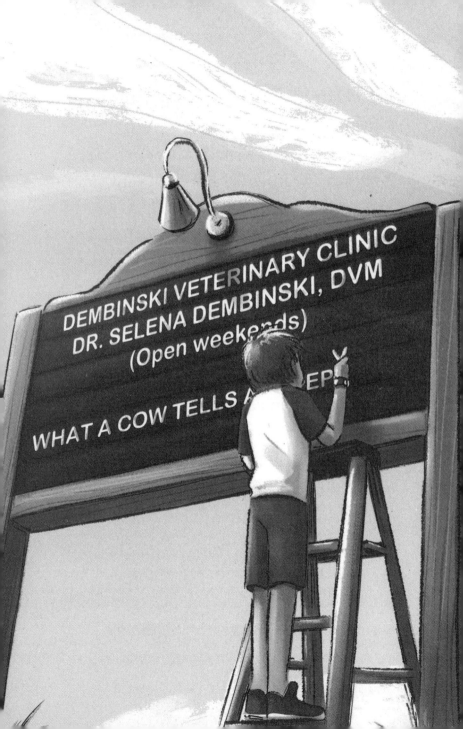

He wanted to be alone so he could work hard.

When he reached his work area, Amy was waiting for him. Popping gum. She held a box, its lid closed. A pair of leather gloves lay on top of the lid.

"Your mom gave me this," Amy said. "Guess what animal is inside?"

"An elephant," Charlie said.

"Ha," Amy said. "It's nice to learn you have a sense of humor. I think you'll be interested in seeing what's inside."

Charlie was curious. But if he let her know that, she'd come around more often to interrupt him.

"You take care of the box. I have work to do."

"Okay," Amy said. "By the way, I finished my cathouse, so I can help you finish your doghouse. What do you think?"

Charlie took a look. The walls of the cathouse tilted at crazy angles, and none of the boards lined up evenly. His mom always told him to say only nice things. But he couldn't think of anything nice to say about a cathouse made so badly.

"You *did* finish it," he said. It was the only truthful thing he could think of. "Congratulations."

Amy popped her gum. "Looks horrible. Maybe there is something to planning things out. Next time. Maybe. When you're done your doghouse, could you help me build a nice-looking cathouse? To sell? I need the money for something important."

"Maybe later." Charlie picked up the power drill from the ground where she had left it. It would be good to get his earplugs in.

"Or maybe I can learn by helping you with your doghouse."

Charlie took a deep breath. This was his project. He liked doing it his way.

"How about for now I help you with what's inside the box," he said.

It could have a cobra in it, but dealing with that would be better than letting Amy mess with his doghouse.

She lifted the lid. An owl stood motionless at the bottom of the box. Charlie knew by its yellow beak and brown eyes that it was a barred owl. A cloth strip was tied around its head. Its entire body was covered in what looked like brown ribbon.

"Somebody dropped it off," Amy said. "They found it in their barn. All that sticky ribbon is flypaper. The owl must have flown into a hanging strip, started flapping and got wrapped up in it. Your mom wants us to try to cut away the flypaper without pulling any feathers loose."

"We'll need to wear the gloves," Charlie said. "And don't—"

Too late. Amy had pulled the cloth off the owl's head. The owl screeched and snapped.

"Ouch!" Amy said. The owl had bitten her thumb.

It continued to struggle against the flypaper and finally fell over. Charlie put the lid back on the box. The owl thumped around inside, then eventually calmed.

"The cloth was a blindfold," Charlie explained to Amy. "When the owl can't see, it can't fight."

Amy's thumb was bleeding. "Rule 45," Charlie said. More than once someone had brought in an injured bird of prey. "Never get in the way of an owl wearing a blindfold."

"Nice to know." Amy winced. "Let's help this poor bird. Then I'll run and get a Band-Aid."

"How about you wear the gloves and hold it," Charlie said. "I'll put the blindfold over its eyes again."

They opened the box.

Amy reached in with protected hands and wrapped her fingers around the owl's wings. Charlie was impressed at the gentle way she held the owl.

After he got the blindfold back on the owl, Amy slowly turned the bird as Charlie peeled away the strips of flypaper.

"It's okay, little guy," Amy whispered. "It's okay."

Charlie didn't want to admit it, but he liked the sound of Amy's voice.

He worked carefully, and the tape came off easily, but the owl's feathers were sticky. Some were clumped together. Charlie's mother had once rescued a sparrow from a glue board meant to trap a mouse, so he knew what to do. First he made sure that the owl's important flight feathers were undamaged. Then he got a bottle of mineral oil from the workshop, poured it onto a cloth and wiped down the owl. The glue lifted. The feathers separated.

"Your mom said we could release the owl by the fence over there," Amy said. "It lives in those woods."

She cradled the owl to her chest. Charlie followed her to the fence, where she set the bird on top of a post.

Slowly she removed the blindfold, then pulled her gloved hands away from the owl's body.

The owl blinked. It shook and fluffed its feathers. Finally, with a low, long hoot, it whooshed into the air and flew directly to the trees.

"Wow!" Amy exclaimed.

"A job well done," Charlie said.

Amy handed Charlie her gloves. "See you later. I need a Band-Aid. Good luck with your doghouse!"

As Amy headed to the clinic, Charlie noticed a pocket-sized notebook on the ground by the crazy-looking cathouse.

Messy writing across the front spelled out AMY'S RULES.

Charlie couldn't help himself. He flipped the book open.

Rule number 1: Dogs don't care so much about what you say. They care about how you say it. Talk to people the same way.

Amy had used the whole page. She had drawn a dog, some hearts and some flowers.

She wouldn't be able to get a lot of rules into the book if she kept using that much space for each rule, Charlie thought. Plus she didn't need the word *number* in there.

He flipped to the second page. He expected to see the second rule. Instead he saw this:

A PLAN TO SAVE DUKE

1. Build and sell cathouse.

2. Ride bicycle to animal shelter and pay for Duke with money from selling cathouse.

3. Take Duke home. He is so cute, Mom won't send him back.

Below this was a row of numbers, some of them scratched out.

~~14~~ ~~13~~ ~~12~~ ~~11~~ ~~10~~ ~~9~~ ~~8~~ ~~7~~ 6 5 4 3 2 1

Charlie gave that some thought. Fourteen. That was how many days an animal was allowed to stay in the shelter. It had been a week since Duke had been there. So *that* was why Amy had said she was running out of time. She needed the money to rescue Duke in case no one adopted the puppy.

As he gave this more thought, his phone beeped.

A text. From his mom. **Time to take Oscar home.**

Chapter Eleven

Selena parked the truck in front of Mrs. Alred's house. Charlie and Amy and Selena lifted the wagon out of the back.

Charlie patted Oscar's head. He whispered in the tone of voice that Amy had used with the owl, "You are a smelly, ugly, rotten dog."

Oscar thumped his tail.

Hmm, Charlie thought. Maybe Amy was right. It was all in *how* you said things.

As they walked toward the house, Mrs. Alred opened the door. "Oscar!" she shouted. "Oscar!"

Oscar barked. It was a happy bark. He pushed himself up onto his front paws. Slowly he made it up onto his back legs.

"Help him out of the wagon," Selena said to Charlie and Amy. "It looks like he's ready to walk."

Mrs. Alred hurried down the front steps. "Oscar!"

Charlie tried to hold Oscar back, but the old dog couldn't wait. Oscar barked again and jumped out of the wagon. He leaned to one side, looking as though he was going to fall, but then he took another step forward, toward Mrs. Alred.

She dropped to her knees and wrapped her arms around Oscar's neck. Oscar licked her face.

"Selena, I couldn't believe it when you phoned me with the good news," Mrs. Alred said. "It was a tick?"

"Yes. The tick caused a rare but serious condition," Selena said. "Female ticks release a type of poison into a dog's bloodstream while they are feeding. Some dogs develop paralysis, and it can lead to death. Ticks can be difficult to find in a dog's fur. The specialist looked but must have missed it. Fortunately, at the clinic, Amy felt it. As soon as we removed the tick, Oscar started to improve."

Oscar thumped his tail again at the mention of his name.

Mrs. Alred stood. "I'm so glad he's home."

Charlie looked at Amy. Amy looked at him. Amy and Charlie looked at Selena. Selena nodded. It was time to announce their plan. Charlie had come up with it. They had talked about it all the way to Mrs. Alred's house.

"Maybe Amy and I could come over more often and try to take Oscar on longer walks," Charlie said. "The more exercise Oscar gets, the healthier he can be."

"That would be nice," Mrs. Alred answered. "Sometimes I can't always go on long walks. Exercise would certainly help him, wouldn't it?"

"He is such a wise, well-behaved dog," Amy said. "Walking him would be easy for us."

"He *is* well behaved," Selena said. She turned to Mrs. Alred. "A younger dog could learn a thing or two by

spending time with Oscar. Charlie had an idea about that."

"I'm getting money from selling a doghouse I built," Charlie said. "I'd like to use the money to adopt a puppy from the animal shelter. Would you let the puppy stay here for a while with Oscar? They could run around together, and Oscar would get even more exercise. I'll pay for the puppy's food. And when the puppy has learned from Oscar not to bark and jump and get too excited, then the puppy can live with us at the clinic."

"I'll stop by every day to help," Amy said. "I don't mind riding a bicycle this far."

Mrs. Alred laughed. "You think I don't know what you are doing here? You're trying to get me to fall in love with a puppy so that when Oscar is gone someday, I will have another friend to keep me company."

"Mrs. Alred," Selena said. "I am shocked, just shocked, that you would accuse us of that." Then Selena laughed. "Charlie and Amy, I told you we wouldn't be able to fool Mrs. Alred."

"It's a good idea though," Mrs. Alred said. "I need some time to think about it."

"Of course," Selena said.

"But only as much time as it takes to make tea," Mrs. Alred said. She smiled. "And I already know the answer is yes."

Chapter Twelve

Two days later Charlie and Amy visited Mrs. Alred. They found her in her fenced backyard, sitting in a lawn chair in the shade of a sun umbrella. Oscar snoozed nearby, in the shade of a big tree. Little Duke was curled into a ball, sleeping against Oscar's chest.

Charlie and Amy each sat in a lawn chair beside Mrs. Alred.

"Nice to see both of you," Mrs. Alred said. "Tea and cookies?"

Charlie rubbed his wrist where he normally wore a watch. He had decided that when he visited Mrs. Alred, he would do his best not to worry about time or his checklist. He had also decided that the only way to make that possible was to leave his watch at home.

"That would be great, Mrs. Alred," he said.

"Charlie. Please. Call me Dorothy."

She headed into the house.

"A nut for a jar of tuna," Charlie said.

"Huh?" Amy answered.

It was fun for Charlie to see her as confused as she sometimes made him feel.

"I'll repeat it for you," Charlie said. "Except I'll say it backward. A nut for a jar of tuna."

It took a second. Then she giggled. "Nice palindrome!"

Charlie liked it when she giggled. He liked it a lot.

Amy leaned back in her chair. "Charlie, I am so happy you used your doghouse money to help me with this. I promise I'll build a nice cathouse, sell it and pay you back."

"That's okay," Charlie said, leaning back in his chair. "It was worth every penny to see how happy Duke was to get out of that cage at the animal shelter. Besides, I'm not sure if you could ever build a nice cathouse."

Amy laughed. "Why doesn't it make me mad when you insult me like that?"

"Because of how I say it," Charlie said.

"What? You read my notebook! Shame on you."

But she said it with a smile. That's when Charlie realized that maybe she

had left the notebook beside her crazy cathouse on purpose, just so he would read it.

Before he could ask, however, she popped her gum.

"So," she said. "Charlie, I still need to know. Did you actually step in pig poop?"

Author's Note

I hope you enjoyed the story as much as I enjoyed learning about life in a veterinary clinic before I began writing it. The situations that Amy and Charlie face in *Pasture Bedtime* are all based on true stories, including the cow that looked like it had climbed a tree. If you ever become a veterinarian someday, who knows what kind of fun true stories you'll be able to share about the animals that you help!

Don't miss out on more great books by Sigmund Brouwer with the JUSTINE McKEEN series

Justine's trying to save the planet,
one person and one cause at a time.